創新開拓

Anne Schraff

Development: Kent Publishing Services, Inc.
Design and Production: Signature Design Group, Inc.

Photo Credits: pages 11, 45, 48, 64, Zuma Press;
page 27, KPA Photo Archive
Photo Credits: pages 96, 116, 125, Library of Congress

書　　名：創新開拓 Albert Einstein and Charles Lindbergh

作　　者：Anne Schraff

責　　編：黃家麗　王朴真

封面設計：張　毅

出　　版：商務印書館 (香港) 有限公司
　　　　　香港筲箕灣耀興道 3 號東滙廣場 8 樓
　　　　　http://www.commercialpress.com.hk

發　　行：香港聯合書刊物流有限公司
　　　　　香港新界大埔汀麗路 36 號中華商務印刷大廈 3 字樓

印　　刷：中華商務彩色印刷有限公司
　　　　　香港新界大埔汀麗路 36 號中華商務印刷大廈 14 字樓

版　　次：2012 年 10 月第 1 版第 1 次印刷
　　　　　©2012 商務印書館 (香港) 有限公司
　　　　　ISBN 978 962 07 1975 2
　　　　　Printed in Hong Kong

版權所有　不得翻印

CONTENTS 目錄

Part 2
Charles Lindbergh 查理斯‧林白

Exercises   練習

Publisher's Note
出版說明

　　繼出版以漫畫為主的 Graphic Biography 系列後，商務印書館推出 Biographies 系列。新系列從 TIME magazine 二十世紀最具影響力的名人中，精選了不同領域的十位名人，有科學家愛因斯坦、前美國總統羅斯福、民權領袖馬丁‧路德‧金，還有勇於突破局限的海倫‧凱勒。

　　Biographies 系列經 Saddleback Educational Publishing 授權出版。本系列增加 Cultural Note（文化知識點），介紹相關社會背景；附帶練習題，可供讀者掌握生詞和英語語法點。

　　"淺顯易懂、啟發心智" 是為特點。我們衷心希望，本系列能為初級英語程度的讀者提供閱讀和學習的樂趣。

商務印書館（香港）有限公司

編輯出版部

Usage Note
使用說明

Step 1

通讀傳記故事。遇到生詞可即時參考註釋。若不明白故事背景，可閱讀文化知識點。

Step 2

完成練習題。若未能回答練習題，或回答錯誤時，可再查閱傳記相關內容。通過練習熟悉生詞意義和用法，掌握語法知識。

Step 3

閱讀中英對照生詞表，檢查是否已掌握生詞。尚未掌握的生詞，可重新閱讀傳記相關部分。

Step 4

閱讀人物年表，重溫傳記故事。讀者可模仿年表，用簡單詞句概括重要事件，練習撮要技巧。

Step 5

延伸閱讀列出有參考價值的相關書籍，讀者可按興趣深入閱讀。

Part 1

Albert Einstein
艾拔・愛因斯坦

A curious boy 樂於求索

In the 17th century, the scientist Sir Isaac Newton taught about space, matter, and time. He taught that space, matter, and time are separate from each other. Albert Einstein came along[1] over 200 years later. He disagreed. He said all three are closely related, or relative to each other. They are connected. And they are connected in ways that can be hard to understand.

---

1   come along: 出現

Einstein turned the world of science upside down[1] with his theory of relativity*. Einstein knew his ideas could play a part in the making of atomic bombs. He wanted them to be used as a force for peace. But he cried out in sorrow when atomic bombs took thousands of lives at the end of World War II.

Albert Einstein was born on Friday, March 14, 1879, in Ulm, Germany. The Einsteins were a middle class[2] family. They had lived in southern Germany for over 300 years. Albert's father, Hermann, was a warm and optimistic[3] man. He was an engineer whose many business ventures[4] had failed. But he never stopped trying. Hermann Einstein married Pauline Koch, a gentle and intelligent young woman, in 1876. The Einsteins were Jews, but they did follow Hebrew

*Cultural Note

theory of relativity：相對論，是關於時空和引力的理論。在愛因斯坦的相對論裏，不存在一個絕對的時間。兩個相對運動的人，他們對各自時間的測量是不同的。

---

1   turn…upside down: 帶來革新
2   middle class: 中產階層
3   optimistic, *adj*: 樂觀
4   venture, *n*: 經營項目

religious practices. For example, they did not go to the synagogue[1] or follow dietary[2] laws*.

Albert was the Einstein's first child. Pauline thought her baby son's head was an unusual shape. She worried that he might have mental problems. Her worry only increased when Albert was slow to learn to speak.

In 1880 the Einsteins moved to Munich, the capital of Bavaria and a center of industry. Albert's father hoped he'd have better luck there. In 1881 Albert's sister, Maja, was born. It was a happy home. The parents showered their two children with love. Grandparents, aunts, and uncles all interested in their well-being surrounded the children. Still, Albert was very quiet. Even at nine, he only spoke slowly and thoughtfully.

*Cultural Note

dietary laws：飲食戒律，此處特指猶太教的相關戒律。根據猶太教習慣，允許教徒食用偶蹄（每隻腳有偶數個腳趾）的反芻動物，禁食昆蟲、食腐動物、爬行動物、兩棲動物和無鰭、無鱗的水產。

1　synagogue, *n*: 猶太教堂
2　dietary, *adj*: 與飲食有關

Albert Einstein was a curious young boy.
艾拔・愛因斯坦童年時期好奇心很強。

When Albert was very young, his father gave him a magnetic compass. The little boy was delighted and captivated[1] by the compass. He kept studying it and turning it around and around. Albert also enjoyed doing jigsaw puzzles[2] and building very high houses of cards. He liked to read, but he never chose light, funny books. He always wanted serious books that he could learn from.

As a young child, Albert was tutored at home. He had a very hot temper[3]. One day, when he was frustrated, he picked up a chair and threw it at his tutor. The angry teacher fled, never to return. Albert learned to control his temper after that.

One day, Albert's parents took him to see a military parade[4]. They thought he would enjoy seeing the marching

---

1 captivate, *v*: 吸引
2 jigsaw puzzle: 拼圖
3 hot temper: 急躁的脾氣
4 military parade: 閱兵

soldiers and hearing the music. But Albert wept at the sight of the soldiers marching close together. They looked like a frightening monster with many arms and legs to the little boy. All his life, Albert would dislike the military.

Albert's mother was a talented[1] pianist who passed on her love of music to her children. Albert loved to listen to his mother playing the piano.

Finally, it was time for Albert to attend regular school. His parents wanted to pick the best school they could find for their son. The nearest good school was a Catholic school. It had a fine academic record. The Einsteins did not care what religion was taught at the school. They only wanted their son to get a good education.

---

1   talented, *adj*: 有才能

Albert Einstein enjoyed hearing the colourful[1] Bible stories at the Catholic school. He was the only Jewish[2] child in the whole school, but that was not a problem. The problem was that Albert just did not like school. He thought it had been better before with a tutor and his parents teaching him at home.

---

1   colourful, *adj*: 生動，美 colorful
2   Jewish, *adj*: 猶太人

CHAPTER 2

Pursuing freedom 嚮往自由

Albert did not like the discipline[1] of the classroom. He did not want to sit in one place. He did not want to do as he was told. He was rebellious and troublesome. He hated having to memorize. Albert preferred being alone, so he avoided the other children. He also disliked sports. He did not take part in[2] any of the games.

---

1 discipline, *n*: 紀律
2 take part in: 參與

Even though seven-year-old Albert did not like school, he worked hard. His report cards[1] were excellent. But Albert always believed he learned the really important things at home. For example, his Uncle Jakob introduced him to algebra. He loved it from the beginning. Whenever the boy had some free time, he studied mathematics on his own. Albert also learned to play the violin at home. His love of music grew.

When he was ten years old, Albert was sent to Luitpold School, a secondary school. Again, he was very unhappy. He knew a lot more than the other students about mathematics and science. He was not popular with[2] the other students. Albert began teaching himself physics[3] and higher mathematics while studying the regular subjects at Luitpold.

---

1 report card: 成績單
2 popular with: 受歡迎
3 physics, *n*: 物理學

To young Albert, school felt like the army. The teachers were like officers. He was told that he had to be like everybody else. He begged his father to move the family out of Germany.

Albert Einstein believed in pacifist[1] ideals from a young age. He worried that he might be drafted[2] into the German army. He believed that all conflicts between nations could be settled by peaceful compromise. He thought war was barbaric[3].

In 1894 when Albert was fifteen, his father failed in business again. Albert's father got a new job in Italy. The family packed up and left Germany. They took their daughter, Maja, with them. Since Albert had not yet graduated from high school, he was left behind. Albert was crushed. He had to live in a boarding house. He was miserable without his family.

---

1 pacifist, *n*: 和平主義者
2 draft, *v*: 徵兵
3 barbaric, *adj*: 殘忍

After six months, Albert quit school and joined his family in Italy. His parents were upset that their son had left school without earning his high school diploma. It was impossible to enter most colleges without a high school diploma.

Albert loved Italy. He went to art galleries. He learned to sail. He climbed mountains. He listened to music. But his parents wanted him to earn a living[1] in electrical engineering. He needed a university degree. Few universities enrolled students without their high school diploma. But his parents found one that required only that students pass an entrance test. It was called the Swiss Federal Polytechnic Institute*. Albert scored well in math but didn't pass the general knowledge test.

*Cultural Note

Swiss Federal Polytechnic Institute：瑞士蘇黎世聯邦工業學院，投考這所以物理、化學、數學聞名的學校未必需要正規中學履歷。沒完成中學教育的愛因斯坦，第二次應考該校入學試時獲取錄。

---

1   earn a living: 謀生

The Institute sent Albert to school for a year in Aarau, a nearby town. There he prepared for the exam. Albert enjoyed school in Switzerland. He loved the land and the people. He felt free to study. He did not just have to memorize dates and facts. He took the test again, and this time he passed.

CHAPTER 3

Struggling for a job 求職艱難

Einstein planned to teach math and physics in high school. He began a four-year course at the Institute. He liked college better than high school. But he was still not a good student. He often cut classes. And he argued with his teachers when he disagreed with them.

Einstein enjoyed walking in the hills around the school. He liked to eat his meals in restaurants. In the evenings, he played music. Einstein and his friends each played an instrument. They would gather at someone's home or in a little coffee shop. Einstein played the violin and a young female student from Serbia, Mileva Maric, played the piano.

Young Albert took notice of the dark haired, dark-eyed Maric, and they became friends. But even though he enjoyed his friends, Einstein was most interested in self-study. He was constantly wondering about the rules of physics and trying to work out problems that interested him. When he and his friends went on sailing boat[1] rides, everyone relaxed. But Einstein wrote math problems and solutions on a notepad[2]. His mind was always busy.

Einstein became a close friend of another student, Marcel Grossman. Einstein and Grossman and other friends spent hours discussing mathematical problems.

---

1   sailing boat: 帆船，美 sailboat
2   notepad, *n*: 記事本

Although Einstein was recognized at the Institute as brilliant and gifted[1], he was unpopular with the professors. He was stubborn. He refused to listen to them and give them the respect they felt they deserved. In August 1900 Einstein graduated. Now twenty-one, he needed a job badly. He was living on an allowance from home, and his family was far from[2] rich. Hermann Einstein never found a good enough position to give his family a worry free life. Albert Einstein wanted to be on his own and not add to the financial burdens of his family.

Einstein wrote letters to different schools asking for a position teaching mathematics. Since he had not made friends with his professors at the Institute, there were no helping hands reaching out to him. On his job applications, Einstein wrote that he had

1   gifted, *adj*: 有天賦
2   far from: 遠非

already published scientific articles in the *German Annals*[1] *of Physics*. But after searching for a year he still had no job. He earned some money tutoring students in math and science. He took part time positions teaching when the regular teachers were ill. But he had no real job and no decent[2] income.

In 1901 Albert Einstein became a citizen of Switzerland. He submitted a paper he had written to the University of Zurich* in the hopes of getting his Ph.D. Such a degree would have increased his chances of finding work. His paper was rejected. Einstein was beginning to feel that the world was against him.

Down to his last few cents, Einstein got a long-term substitute teaching job at Winterthur, 17 miles north of Zurich. He taught mathematics to boys

*Cultural Note

University of Zurich：蘇黎世大學，成立於 1833 年，是瑞士最大的大學。在瑞士所有高等院校中，蘇黎世大學提供的課程最多樣、最全面。

1   annals, *n*: 活動年報
2   decent, *adj*: 足夠

who were not interested at first. But Einstein discovered that he was able to gain their attention and teach them something. But that job ended and soon Einstein was so poor that he was cutting back on[1] his meals and losing weight. He got another job tutoring boys, but he was fired when his employer disagreed with his methods.

Albert Einstein had almost given up hope of finding a good job. In 1902 his friend, Marcel Grossman, came to his rescue.

---

1 cut back on: 减少

Theory of Relativity 相對論

With the help of his friend, Marcel Grossman, Albert Einstein got a job in Bern, Switzerland, at the patent[1] office* as a third class examiner. His job was to be part of a technical team looking at new inventions and deciding if they deserved a patent. A patent is a document certifying that the invention worked and was original. Einstein loved to work with[2] new inventions. He was like a child again, staring with wonder at that compass[3] his father gave him. Einstein's

*Cultural Note

the patent office in Bern, Switzerland：愛因斯坦是在瑞士伯爾尼一家專利局當初級研究員的時候研究出相對論的。為了維持家計，他在專利局工作，專門分析其他人的發明。

---

1 patent, *adj*: 專利
2 work with: 從事…工作
3 compass, *n*: 指南針

skill and enthusiasm soon got him promoted to second class technical expert.

Mileva Maric was a physicist[1] like Albert Einstein. She too had big dreams for her profession. She enjoyed discussing scientific theories with Einstein. She was intelligent enough to understand him. Originally from Greece with Serbian roots[2], she grew up in Hungary. Four years older than Einstein, she was bright, energetic, and quick. But Albert Einstein wanted a wife, not a partner in his work. He asked Maric to marry him. They were married in January 1903.

The young couple rented an apartment with a view of the Alps. Einstein was pondering[3] the nature of light, concluding that it was made up of individual particles of energy, which he

---

1   physicist, *n*: 物理學家
2   root, *n*: 原籍
3   ponder, *v*: 琢磨

called photons. The scientific world at the time thought light was transmitted in waves.

Albert Einstein with his wife, Mileva Maric.
艾拔・愛因斯坦和夫人米列娃・馬利奇。

The Einstein's first son, Hans Albert, was born on May 14, 1904. Einstein was very happy as a father. He often wheeled his infant son down the street in a baby carriage. He even tried to help his wife with the household chores[1]. Mileva Einstein was a perfectionist. Soon, she was taking care of the baby and the house while Einstein was writing scientific articles and thinking about atoms[2] and molecules[3]. At the time, no one knew for sure if atoms and molecules even existed.

Atoms and molecules are the smallest particles in nature. They are often invisible, even under a microscope. Einstein wanted to prove that these invisible particles behaved just like larger, visible particles. He noticed that larger particles moved around when in a liquid. He thought they were being hit

---

1   chore, *n*: 零工
2   atom, *n*: 原子
3   molecule, *n*: 分子

by smaller, invisible particles. The only way to prove his theory was through mathematics.

The motion of particles was called Brownian Motion[1]. Einstein published an article, "On the Movement of Small Particles," in 1905. He proved the existence of molecules and their motion. For this discovery, Albert Einstein was awarded a Doctor of Philosophy degree from the University of Zurich.

1905 was an incredible year for Einstein. It came to be called a "Wonderful Year." He published a number of research papers that changed science forever. While working full time at the patent office, he produced revolutionary theories about space, matter, and time.

Einstein turned his attention to the study of light. The speed of light had

---

1   Brownian Motion: 布朗運動

been verified[1] as 186,000 miles a second. Now Einstein concluded that the speed of light in free space was the only fixed thing in the universe. Everything else is relative. This was called his "Theory of Relativity."

According to Einstein, time is variable. For example, if someone walked beside a man bouncing a ball, the path of the ball would look straight up and down. But if you stood still, and the man walked past you bouncing the ball, the ball would appear to move diagonally up and down. So it would seem as if the ball went a longer distance in the same amount of time. The idea of time and space, then, depended on the observer and where he was.

Another example is a sailor raising a flag on a ship. To the sailor standing at the base of the flagpole, the flag moves

---

1 verify, *v*: 證實

straight up. But to an observer on shore, the flag moves forward and up at the same time. Time and space are relative. They depend on the observer's frame of reference.

Einstein published his article on special relativity in the *Annals of Physics*. When other scientists read it, some were upset. They thought this twenty-six-year-old upstart[1] was tampering with[2] Isaac Newton's* fixed laws. Others, however, knew Einstein's insights were important. They increased our understanding of the universe.

*Cultural Note

Isaac Newton： 艾薩克・牛頓（1643-1727），萬有引力定律的提出者，經典力學的奠基人，和另一位科學家萊布尼茲各自獨立地發明了微積分。

1　upstart, *n*: 傲慢的新人
2　tamper with: 擾亂

CHAPTER 5

Rose to fame 聲名鵲起

*Cultural Note

e=mc² : 根 據 愛 因 斯
坦 的 方 程 式 e=mc²，
物 質 能 夠 轉 換 成 能
量，能 量 也 能 轉 換
成 物 質。迄 今 為 止，
e=mc² 已 被 多 次 使
用，如 應 用 為 製 造 原
子 彈 提 供 理 論 基 礎。

Albert Einstein then began to think about energy and matter. Einstein said they are different forms of the same thing. His idea was that if matter moved fast enough, it became energy. If energy was slowed down, it became matter. He introduced a mathematical equation to prove this theory: $E = mc^2$*. "E" stands for energy, "m" stands for mass, and "c^2" stands for the speed of light multiplied by itself. The equation says that there is a huge amount of energy tied up in even a small amount of matter. For the first time, someone explained how the sun could go on giving off light for billions of years without cooling off[1].

Albert Einstein came up with[2] these amazing ideas when he was still a clerk at the patent office. His friends told him that with his knowledge, he should be a university professor. But Einstein feared having teaching responsibilities. He thought teaching would take too much time from his research.

Einstein was receiving invitations to lecture at universities. Mileva Einstein was hoping for a better career for her husband. Einstein enjoyed work at the patent office. But he wondered if he would always be happy looking at new inventions.

---

1   cool off: 冷却
2   come up with: 提出

In 1909 Albert Einstein became a professor of physics at the University of Zurich. Albert and Mileva Einstein fell in love with Zurich. It was a happy time for the family. Albert Einstein enjoyed playing games and telling stories to his five-year-old son. Albert and Mileva often attended the opera and the theatre. On July 28, 1910, the Einstein's second son was born. Eduard was given the pet nickname of "Tete." Unlike the robust[1] Hans, Eduard was a frail[2] child.

With the birth of a second child, Mileva Einstein believed the family needed more money. Einstein added more lectures. He began thinking about the problems of gravity. In 1911 Einstein was offered a higher salary to teach at the University of Prague. Soon, Albert Einstein's fame spread. He was

---

1 robust, *adj*: 強壯
2 frail, *adj*: 虛弱

invited to meetings with world famous scientists. Then Einstein was offered three jobs, director of physics at the prestigious[1] Kaiser Wilhelm Institute, membership in the Prussian[2] Academy of Science, and professor at the University of Berlin.

News that the family might be moving to Germany made Mileva Einstein very unhappy. Einstein accepted the new jobs. Mileva Einstein and her two sons continued to live in Switzerland. The marriage was over. She had been unhappy for a long time because her own career as a physicist never developed. She was frustrated with her husband's personality.

Mileva Einstein began a new life as a divorcée[3] and single mother with two young boys. Albert Einstein supported his family financially. He made regular

---

1   prestigious, *adj*: 有聲望

2   Prussian, *adj*: 普魯斯

3   divorcée, *n*: 離婚者

trips to Switzerland to see his sons. But he was very lonely living alone in Berlin.

To relieve his loneliness, Einstein often visited his Uncle Rudolf who lived in Berlin. Rudolf Einstein's daughter, Elsa, lived there as well with her two daughters, Margot and Ilse. Albert Einstein and Elsa Einstein were cousins. They had often played together as children. He felt very comfortable with her. He liked the two girls, too. When Albert played the violin and Elsa played the piano, the girls were charmed.

Einstein found he liked living in Berlin. The people were friendlier than he expected. He spent much of his time studying gravity[1]. He also spent pleasant hours with Elsa and her daughters. Like Einstein, Elsa was also divorced. She scolded Albert for not taking better care of himself. He seemed much too thin.

---

1 gravity, *n*: 重力

Unlike Mileva, Elsa was not a brilliant woman. She was simple, kind, and down to earth[1]. Little by little, she became an important part of Albert Einstein's life.

But another dark cloud was looming[2] over the life of Einstein and all of Europe. In 1914 it appeared that the world would soon be going to war.

---

1   down to earth: 務實
2   loom, *v*: 逼近

CHAPTER 6

A pacifist 熱愛和平

Albert Einstein hated war. He was a pacifist. He joined with other scientists in pleading with Europeans to start a league dedicated to[1] peace. Einstein began to promote peace, tolerance, and justice. He was horrified by the thought of Europe being torn apart by war. But by the end of the summer of 1914, full-scale war raged[2]. Injuries and death mounted on both sides. Einstein saw it as senseless evil.

---

1   dedicate to: 專注於…

2   rage, *v*: 猛烈持續

Einstein still worked on his new ideas about space, matter, and time. He wanted to show how gravity fit with his ideas. After eight years of work, he concluded that gravity was the product of space distorted by the presence of matter. In 1916 Einstein published his ideas as the "General Theory of Relativity." This has been called his most important achievement.

Einstein said that a beam of light would be bent by gravity as it passed a star. The gravity of the star would cause the light beam to curve. In 1919 Einstein's theory was tested. British astronomers photographed stars during a total eclipse of the sun[1]. The photographs were compared with pictures of the same stars when the sun was far off. The different positions of the stars on the two different photographs proved that the sun deflects[2] starlight.

---

1 total eclipse of the sun: 日全食
2 deflect, *v*: 使轉向

Einstein's general theory of relativity helped explain such things as the curved shape of the universe. It also explained why the universe is expanding, what black holes are, and the "big bang[1]" theory of how the universe began.

In 1919 five months after his divorce to Mileva Einstein was final, Albert Einstein married Elsa Einstein Lowenthal. Einstein legally adopted Elsa's two daughters. He enjoyed them immensely[2]. Once again, Albert Einstein had a happy home. But he continued to work hard. Elsa tenderly cared for him when he was sick.

Einstein spent a lot of time reading philosophy and listening to music. He worked to discover what is called a unified field theory. Einstein sought to discover a single law that explains how all natural forces work.

---

1   big bang, *n*: 宇宙大爆炸
2   immensely, *adv*: 非常

Einstein continued to see his sons. In 1920 he met fifteen-year-old Hans in Italy. They hiked for several days and Einstein shared fatherly advice.

In 1920 Albert Einstein was the subject of much publicity and admiration. But in Germany, his work was sometimes criticized. Anti-semitism[1] was a terrible problem in Germany. After the end of World War I*, it flared[2] with increased energy. Some Germans, embittered[3] by the fact that they lost World War I, blamed the Jews. They also blamed the Jews for terrible unemployment and inflation in Germany. Einstein's theories were ridiculed as "Jewish physics."

In Germany, there was a small group of angry Germans promoting the idea that only pure "Aryan"[4] Germans were worthy human beings. All non-Aryans,

*Cultural Note

World War I：第一次世界大戰（1914 年 8 月—1918 年 11 月）是一場主要發生在歐洲但波及到全世界的世界大戰，當時世界上大多數國家都捲入了這場戰爭。

---

1   anti-semitism, *n*: 反猶太主義
2   flare, *v*: 加劇
3   embitter, *v*: 激怒
4   Aryan, *adj*: 雅利安人

especially Jews, were belittled[1]. The leader of this violent movement was a former house painter named Adolf Hitler. At that time, hardly anyone suspected the role Hitler would play in the future. But Einstein and other thoughtful men were disgusted and alarmed.

---

1   belittle, *v*: 貶低

CHAPTER 7

American citizenship 入籍美國

In 1921 Chaim Weizmann, a chemistry professor and leader of the Zionist movement* asked for Einstein's help in establishing Hebrew University in Palestine. The Zionists[1] wanted to create a homeland for Jewish people. Einstein accompanied Weizmann on a trip to the United States. The Einsteins arrived in New York in April. Reporters crowded about to interview him.

*Cultural Note

Zionist movement：猶太復國主義運動，是猶太人的政治運動，也指支援猶太人在以色列土地建立家園的意識形態，它很大程度上是對十九世紀時反猶太主義的一種回應。

1　Zionist, *n*: 猶太復國主義者

Albert Einstein was invited to the White House to meet President Franklin Roosevelt. The family was greeted wherever they went with warmth and good will.

Columbia University gave him a medal and offered him a job. Einstein raised[1] millions of dollars for Hebrew University.

Einstein gave a series of lectures at Princeton University. His lectures on the theory of relativity were delivered[2] in German. An American professor then gave the same lecture in English. The lectures were published in a book, *The Meaning of Relativity*. Princeton gave him an honorary degree.

After the U.S. trip, Einstein traveled the world. He met with scientists and gave lectures. During a trip to Japan, he learned that he won the Nobel Prize in physics.

1   raise, *v*: 籌募
2   deliver, *v*: 發表

Einstein demonstrates his formulas on a blackboard during a lecture.
講座時，愛因斯坦在黑板上講解公式。

He was also awarded membership into all of the leading scientific academies.

Meanwhile, trouble was brewing[1] in Germany. The Nazi Party[2]* was gaining in popularity. Even as his fame was growing around the world, Einstein's belief in peace and a unified Europe was not popular at home. Prejudice against Jews made Germany a dangerous place for the Einstein family. Friends begged them to leave the troubled country.

In 1933 the Einsteins moved permanently to the United States. Einstein was invited to become a professor at Princeton University in New Jersey. Einstein's sister, Maja, also came to the United States. Hans Einstein, his son, found work in the United States as an engineer.

*Cultural Note

Nazi Party：納粹黨，民族社會主義德國工人黨的簡稱，前身是德國工人黨。1919年成立於德國，1933年在希特勒領導下得權。1945年，德國在第二次世界大戰中戰敗，納粹黨被解散。

1   brew, *v*: 形成
2   Nazi Party, *n*: 納粹黨

The magnificent campus[1] of Princeton University awed Albert Einstein. When he was asked how he wanted his office furnished, he asked for a desk, a chair, and a waste-paper basket[2] where he could throw his mistakes.

The Einsteins were touched by the kindness of ordinary people. Children approached him everywhere he went. They knew who he was. On Christmas Eve, groups of boys and girls sang carols[3] for the Einsteins. Albert Einstein rushed outside and asked the children if he could get his violin and join them as they made the rounds[4] of the neighborhood. Wearing a leather jacket and stocking cap and playing his violin, Einstein became a caroler that night.

Albert Einstein decided to become a citizen of the United States.

---

1   campus: 校園
2   waste-paper basket: 廢紙筒，美 wastebasket
3   carol, *n*: 聖誕頌歌
4   round, *n*: 巡迴路線

Albert Einstein taking part in a ceremony,
making him a citizen of the United States.
艾拔‧愛因斯坦宣誓成為美國公民。

Letter to Roosevelt 給總統的信

Albert Einstein continued to believe in pacifism[1], but the actions of Adolf Hitler were changing his mind. He was beginning to fear that nothing but military force would stop Hitler.

In the mid-1930s, the Einsteins lived a simple life. They had no car and few luxuries. Einstein gained all the joy he needed listening to music and walking in the woods. In 1936 Elsa Einstein became pale and tired. She refused to go

---

1 pacifism, *n*: 和平主義

to the hospital and nurses cared for her at home. Finally, she grew so ill that Albert Einstein had to hospitalize her. In December 1936 Elsa Einstein died.

Einstein was devastated[1] by the loss of his wife. His loneliness was eased when his stepdaughter, Margot, came to live with him. Einstein and a colleague wrote a book, *Evolution of Physics*, which was published in 1937.

Late in 1939 some Hungarian physicists with alarming news visited Albert Einstein. They believed Adolf Hitler's scientists were close to producing an atomic bomb. They urged Einstein to use his great prestige[2] to convince President Roosevelt to immediately begin work on an American atomic bomb.

1　devastate, *v*: 打擊
2　prestige, *n*: 聲望

Einstein was horrified about urging the development of such a terrible weapon. But he feared that if Hitler developed the bomb first, humanity would be in peril[1]. So he wrote the letter to President Roosevelt describing how an atomic bomb could be produced. President Roosevelt set American scientists to work on the project.

In October 1940 Albert Einstein took the oath of American citizenship. In December 1941 the United States was attacked by Japan at Pearl Harbor, and Einstein's adopted[2] country was fighting for its life. Einstein did everything he could for the war effort. He urged Americans to buy war bonds[3], and he gave advice to the scientists working on the Manhattan Project* to build the atomic bomb.

*Cultural Note

Manhattan Project：曼克頓計劃，是美國於 1942 年開始實施的研製原子彈的計劃。為了先於納粹德國製造出原子彈，該工程集中了當時西方國家最優秀的核科學家，於 1945 年成功地進行了世界上第一次核爆炸。

1   in peril: 處於險境
2   adopted, *adj*: 入籍
3   war bond: 戰時公債

As the war raged on with mounting[1] casualties[2], Einstein mourned. Germany surrendered in May 1945, but the United States was still fighting Japan. Then, in the summer of 1945, Albert Einstein learned of the bombing of Hiroshima[3], Japan. He was told that over sixty thousand people had died in an atomic blast[4]. Many more would die of radiation sickness.

Days later, another atomic bomb was dropped on Nagasaki[5], Japan. About forty thousand lives were lost. Japan surrendered quickly, ending World War II, but Albert Einstein was heartsick. He said if he had known the atomic bomb would be used in this way by the United States he never would have written to President Roosevelt urging atomic research. Einstein tried to believe that he was not directly responsible for the bomb. But for Einstein, the devoted

---

1   mounting, *adj*: 上升

2   casualty, *n*: 傷亡

3   Hiroshima: 廣島

4   blast, *n*: 爆炸

5   Nagasaki: 長崎

pacifist, the horrors of Hiroshima and Nagasaki haunted him. He had always hated war. This was war at its absolute worst.

Einstein looked for a way to turn the pain he was feeling into something useful. He resolved to work diligently[1] for peace so never again would atomic bombs be dropped on a city. He joined with other physicists to ask for a world government with a military force that would make sure World War III would never happen.

After World War II, the Cold War[2] began between the non-communist world of the United States and her allies[3] and the communist[4] world of Russia and her allies. There was great fear of communism throughout the United

---

1   diligently, *adv*: 勤勉
2   Cold War: 冷戰
3   ally, *n*: 聯盟國
4   communist, *n*: 共產主義者

States. Einstein's campaign for peace led some to believe he was leaning toward communism.

Einstein was sorry that he was misunderstood. But he felt compelled to work for peace while he was still working on scientific problems.

Anti-atomic ideal 反原子武器

Albert Einstein had received degrees from universities all over the world. He had so many medals and honors that he lost count. The Einstein Institute of Mathematics at the Hebrew University of Jerusalem* was named for him. Albert Einstein was thought to be one of the most important men in the world.

Einstein continued to think and kept his pad and pencil near for mathematical equations. Einstein

*Cultural Note

Hebrew University of Jerusalem：耶 路 撒 冷希伯來大學，是以色列歷史第二長的大學，也是以色列最優秀的大學之一。愛因斯坦曾任該大學第一屆理事會理事。

always refused to believe that anything in the universe happens purely by chance. He believed that laws govern everything, and he continued to struggle to find those laws.

Einstein campaigned on for world government and for a ban on atomic weapons. He felt sure that atomic weapons posed a threat to the human race.

In 1952 Einstein's old friend and fellow scientist, Chaim Weizmann, the first president of Israel, died. To his astonishment, Einstein was offered Weizmann's job as president of Israel. Some Israelis believed that having Einstein as their president would increase the influence of the new nation. Einstein refused. He could not imagine himself as a politician.

Now seventy-three, Einstein was often caught up in sadness. Many of his old friends had died. He still missed Elsa, his wife. He worried about the health of his beloved stepdaughter, Margot.

Albert Einstein worried about what he saw as moral decay in society. He loved science, but he believed that the struggle for justice and truth was more important than anything else. He said that people can find meaning in life only by promoting good in society.

In his old age, Einstein enjoyed the company of his wire-haired terrier, Chico, and young people. Children often joined him on walks, peppering[1] him with questions. Like the children, Einstein continued to be delighted by the wonders of nature.

---

1 pepper, v: 接連提問

Einstein greatly admired the spiritual leader of India, Mahatma Gandhi. Gandhi, a tireless advocate[1] of nonviolence[2], had done so much for humanity. Gandhi, like Einstein, was a pacifist.

March 14, 1954 was Albert Einstein's seventy-fifth birthday. Tributes poured in from around the world. When he heard the voices of praise, Einstein asked what he had done to deserve this.

A young student asked Einstein what he believed in, and he answered the brotherhood of man. Einstein described science without religion as lame[3], and religion without science as blind.

---

1 advocate, *n*: 提倡者
2 nonviolence, *n*: 非暴力
3 lame, *adj*: 跛

CHAPTER 10

Person of the century 世紀人物

Half a dozen years earlier, Albert Einstein found out he had a serious medical condition—a weak spot in one of his arteries[1]. Einstein ignored this, and in April 1955 he became seriously ill with stomach pain, often a symptom[2] of heart trouble. The family doctor sent for specialists who suggested surgery might be necessary. Einstein refused an operation saying he was too old. But he did agree to enter Princeton Hospital for a few days.

---

1   artery, *n*: 動脈
2   symptom, *n*: 症狀

Albert Einstein referred to death as "the old debt" which all people must pay. He felt his time to pay the debt was close, but he did not want to stay in the hospital. When his son, Hans, came from California, Einstein assured him he was feeling better.

Even while he lay in his hospital bed, Einstein asked that his latest pages of mathematical equations be brought to him so he might add something.

In the very early hours of the morning of April 18, 1955, Einstein began mumbling in German. The nurse who was with him did not understand German so she could not tell anyone what Einstein's last words were. He died before the next day dawned. The weakened artery had apparently burst.

Einstein had known for some time that he was dying and he made plans for it. He wanted no funeral, no grave, and no monument. Albert Einstein was not a religious man. He believed the universe was so awesome that it had to have been created by a supreme intelligence. His name for this creator was "the old gentleman."

Einstein wanted his body cremated[1] with the ashes disposed of secretly. He felt his work was the important thing about his life, and he did not want his earthly remains to be the center of attention.

He did permit his brain to be removed during an autopsy[2]. Scientists wanted to discover if there was anything unusual about the brain of a genius. They did find that the part of Einstein's brain associated with mathematical reasoning,

---

1   cremate, *v*: 火化
2   autopsy, *n*: 驗屍

the inferior parietal[1], was fifteen percent wider on both sides than normal.

Albert Einstein was considered to be one of the world's rare geniuses, as Isaac Newton was in his time.

Fame and popularity meant nothing to Einstein. In fact, they often distressed him. He had little use for wealth or material goods. He continued to be amazed that people needed so many things to make them happy. He was a humble, patient, and dedicated[2] man. His joy was derived from observing nature and finding scientific truths.

*Time** magazine voted Albert Einstein the person who made the most important contributions to the 20th century. Einstein himself would not have agreed. He always mourned[3] the victims of the atomic bomb and feared a

1   inferior parietal: 下頂葉
2   dedicated, *adj*: 專注
3   mourn, *v*: 哀悼

future world war that might destroy the world he loved so much. In the end, Albert Einstein's determination to work for human brotherhood and world peace was perhaps as important as his revolutionary ideas about space, matter, and time.

Albert Einstein is regarded by many as the most important scientist of the 20th century and the greatest physicist of all time.

許多人認為艾拔・愛因斯坦是二十世紀最重要的科學家和人類歷史上最偉大的物理學家。

Exercises 練習

I Vocabulary 詞彙

I.I Word ladders 字梯

根據 Albert Einstein 一書填空，改變上一個單詞中的一到三個字母，寫出下一個單詞。

an instrument to find direction	_____
something to sleep on	matter
something that occupies space	_____
the person who is "at bat"	_____
	light
the opposite of dark	_____
not loose	_____
something a watch tells	_____
to crawl up using hands and feet	_____
a country in Asia	_____
below the mouth	violin
a stringed instrument	_____
to break a law	_____
	path
a small trail	_____
short for mathematics	_____
to put together	_____
an error	_____

1.2 Word Scramble 拼字遊戲

請閱讀以下單詞的定義，重新排列字母，寫出書中的原詞。

		Unscrambled Word	Synonym or Related Word
1.	an idea that has been scientifically tested—**rytoeh**	_____	_____
2.	related to each other—**alerveti**	_____	_____
3.	the science of matter, energy, and motion—**ycsphi**	_____	_____
4.	a person who is opposed to violence—**ifistpca**	_____	_____
5.	a very small particle—**emolcuel**	_____	_____
6.	to think deeply about—**nodper**	_____	_____
7.	a light particle—**nophto**	_____	_____
8.	not very strong—**ailrf**	_____	_____
9.	a major undertaking—**ctprjoe**	_____	_____
10.	someone who supports a cause—**ctadove**	_____	_____
11.	a sign of an illness—**omtysmp**	_____	_____
12.	part of the body that deals with thought—**barni**	_____	_____
13.	positive-thinking—**ticpomsiit**	_____	_____
14.	an educational institution—**itunvyesri**	_____	_____
15.	a piece of scientific literature—**rtiacl**	_____	_____

Part 2

Charles Lindbergh

查理斯 · 林白

CHAPTER 1

From shy to rugged 磨練心智

Twenty-five-year-old Charles Lindbergh flew a plane alone non-stop across the Atlantic Ocean. This adventure took place on May 21, 1927. His daring[1] journey from New York to Paris was the first flight of this kind in history. The flight brought the world of aviation[2] dramatically into the public eye. Air travel was rare and unusual before this. Lindbergh launched[3] the age of commercial aviation.

Charles Augustus Lindbergh was born on February 4, 1902, in Detroit,

---

1   daring, *adj*: 無畏

2   aviation, *n*: 航空

3   launch, *v*: 開啟

Michigan. His family was Swedish, English, Irish, and Scottish. His mother, Evangeline, was a schoolteacher. His father, Charles, was a lawyer, realtor, and also, a member of the United States House of Representatives*. Evangeline was seventeen years younger than her husband.

Charles was raised in Little Falls, Minnesota along the Mississippi River. The family was wealthy with a cook, a maid, and a coachman[1]. As a baby and small child, Charles spent most of his time outside in the brisk[2] Minnesota weather. His father wanted to toughen him up. He wanted Charles to be a rugged[3] boy.

The Lindberghs raised cattle, hogs, sheep, chickens, horses, and pigeons. Charles always had a dog. He loved dogs all his life. In 1906 when Charles was four, his father was elected to the United

*Cultural Note

United States House of Representatives：美國國會是美國的立法機構，分為參議院（Senate）和眾議院（House of Representatives）。美國國會現有席位 535 個。參議院席位，美國每個州設 2 席，共 100 個。眾議院席位按人口比例選舉產生，現為 435 個。

1　coachman, *n*: 馬車夫
2　brisk, *adj*: 凜冽
3　rugged, *adj*: 健壯

States Congress as a Republican[1]. He was now away from the family for long periods because he worked in Washington, D.C.

Young Charles was very shy. He had no friends, except for his dogs. He loved to collect things. He had collections of stones, arrowheads, cigar bands, coins, and stamps. He was happiest when he was alone with his dog, roaming through the woods or having adventures.

He built a raft and poled[2] himself down the Mississippi in it. He also built stilts and a garden hut behind the house. He was a clever boy. He noticed his mother had a hard time getting ice from the river for her icebox. So, Charles built a series of planks and pulleys[3] to bring chunks[4] of ice from the river right into the family kitchen. Charles loved animals, and he trained a wild chipmunk to be a pet.

---

1   Republican, *n*: 共和黨人
2   pole, *v*: 開船
3   pulley, *n*: 滑輪
4   chunk, *n*: 厚塊

One day, Charles heard the roar of an engine that was different than anything he had heard before. He ran to his bedroom window to see an airplane with two sets of wings flying over the treetops. It was the first plane the five-year-old had ever seen. He was thrilled[1]. The image of that little plane stayed in his mind.

At age seven, Charles got a Savage .22 calibre[2] repeating rifle. He shot a duck fifty feet away. He was an excellent marksman[3]. He swam and fished, and grew into a rugged, self-reliant boy.

Charles's parents were not happy together. But, they did not want to get a divorce for fear of hurting their son. Still, Charles noticed their unhappiness, and it made him sad.

Until he was eight, Charles was home-schooled by his mother. He enjoyed this

---

1   thrill, *v*: 激動
2   calibre, *n*: 口徑，美 caliber
3   marksman, *n*: 神槍手

because he loved being with his mother. She made the lessons exciting. But then he was sent to public school, and he hated it. He disliked the other children. He found the lessons boring. Although he was bright, he did poorly.

In 1913 when Charles was eleven, he was enrolled in a private school—Sidwell Friends School. It was better than public school, but still Charles did not like it. The other children made fun of his name. They called him "limburger cheese," or just "cheese." Charles avoided his classmates and did not join in any games.

Sometimes Charles's father took him to Washington to sit in on the sessions[1] in Congress. Charles saw the president. He was proud that his father was such an important man, making speeches and passing laws.

---

1   session, *n*: 會議

CHAPTER 2

Dream came true 夢想成真

When Charles was twelve, his father took him to the Aeronautical Trials at Ft. Myers, Virginia. Six airplanes took off and landed. Charles watched with great excitement. He made up his mind that day that he would fly a plane someday.

Charles also traveled to the Panama Canal. He saw alligators, monkeys, lizards, tarantulas[1], coral snakes, and sharks. He was delighted to see all the exotic[2] creatures. It was the beginning of his deep love for nature.

---

1   tarantula, *n*: 狼蛛
2   exotic, *adj*: 外國

In 1913 the Lindberghs got a Model T Ford. Charles then learned to drive it. He did exercises to lengthen his legs so he could reach the controls. Soon he was driving all over in the Model T as well as on a motorcycle.

Charles entered Little Falls High School for a while. Then, his mother had to go to California. Although Charles had no driver's license, he drove his mother and himself from Minnesota to California.

They stayed in California, and Charles entered 11th grade at Redondo Union High School in Redondo Beach, California. Mother and son took motor trips all over southern California. Charles loved the ocean beaches.

In 1917 Charles and his mother returned to Little Falls. Fifteen-year-old Charles played a major role in running the farm, bookkeeping, and tending the livestock[1]. Most of the time, his father was in Washington.

At this time, the United States was getting involved in World War I. The war was being fought between England, France, and Russia against Germany and its allies[2].

Charles's father made speeches against American involvement in the war. He believed all wars were stupid and evil. He thought that a country should avoid them at all cost. Charles heard many of his father's bitter speeches against the war. Therefore, these ideas were planted firmly in the boy's mind. As Charles grew older, these attitudes would shape his life.

In his last year of high school, Charles did well in physics and mechanical drawing. But he failed everything else. It

---

1   livestock, *n*: 家畜
2   ally, *n*: 聯盟國

looked like he would not be getting his high school diploma.

Then, the school district announced that because World War I was raging, food products were in desperate need. They said that any boy who went to work on a farm producing food would automatically get his high school diploma.

So in June 1918, Charles's work on the farm gained him his high school diploma. At the time, he was raising chickens and lambs. He was also mending fences, cutting trees, and clearing the land. All the time, he was dreaming of becoming a pilot as soon as he could.

The Lindbergh farm was sold then. Charles Lindbergh enrolled at the University of Wisconsin in Madison,

Wisconsin. Charles's parents were no longer living together. So, his mother moved to Madison, too, while he attended college there.

Once again, Charles Lindbergh disliked his classes and made no friends. The only activity he liked was the Reserve Officers Training Corps*. He became a cadet[1]. He was very good with pistols and rifles. He wrote letters to many flying schools. He hoped to quit college and learn to fly.

In February 1922 he quit college and joined the Nebraska Aircraft Corporation. He worked on planes. Finally, he went on his first flight in a Lincoln Standard Tourabout. He was thrilled to be riding in the cockpit[2], and soon he was a pilot. He found the actual flying and the take off easy. But he had a hard time learning to land smoothly.

1   cadet, *n*: 候補軍官
2   cockpit, *n*: 駕駛室

Lindbergh began doing stunts[1] on the wings of planes. Sometimes he would stand on the wing. His feet would be strapped down, and the pilot would fly loops. Lindbergh earned the name "Daredevil[2] Lindbergh." By mid-May 1922, Lindbergh had eight hours of flying experience in a Fokker biplane[3]. The other pilots nicknamed him "Slim" because he was tall and lanky[4].

Lindbergh wanted to experience jumping from a plane with a parachute. So, in 1922 he got out of the plane at an altitude of about 2,000 feet. He crawled from the cockpit and crept along the wing until he jumped. The parachute blossomed overhead as he sailed down.

Now, Lindbergh wanted his own plane. He set about getting it.

---

1 stunt, *n*: 特技
2 daredevil, *n*: 膽大
3 biplane, *n*: 複翼飛機
4 lanky, *adj*: 瘦長

Crossed the Atlantic 飛越大西洋

Charles Lindbergh saved enough money to buy a 90 horsepower Curtiss Jenny. This plane was capable of going seventy mph (miles per hour). The plane cost five hundred dollars. Lindbergh flew solo in the plane. He almost crash landed! But by the end of the day, he mastered the technique of landing.

In the summer of 1922, Lindbergh flew all over the United States. He took passengers for rides to earn money. In 1926 he became an airmail pilot on the St. Louis to Chicago mail route. He often flew through thick fog and treacherous[1] weather conditions.

Now twenty-five, Lindbergh heard of the Orteig Prize*. Raymond Orteig was a French businessman. He was offering $25,000 to any flier or group of fliers who could cross the Atlantic Ocean from New York to Paris, or Paris to New York non-stop. Lindbergh was excited about the offer. He believed he could do it.

Charles Lindbergh did not have enough money to accomplish[2] this goal. He did not have a plane that could make the journey. So, he looked for financial backers[3]. He spoke to a group of interested men in St. Louis, Missouri. They provided the money.

*Cultural Note

Orteig Prize：1919年，美國紐約酒店主雷蒙德・奧泰格（Raymond Orteig）提供 25,000 美金作為獎賞，鼓勵任何能不停站由紐約飛越大西洋，到達巴黎的飛行員或組別。

---

1 treacherous, *adj*: 危險
2 accomplish, *v*: 實現
3 backer, *n*: 贊助者

Ryan Aircraft Company, a small company in San Diego, California, was chosen to build the plane. The plane would be called the *Spirit of St. Louis* in honor of the backers.

By mid-April 1927, a single engine Ryan monoplane was wheeled out[1] of the Ryan factory. On April 28 at Dutch flats, south of San Diego, Lindbergh took the plane up. For the next two weeks he tested the plane. He cruised[2] at 130 mph On May 10, Lindbergh piloted the *Spirit of St. Louis* to New York to make the historical flight.

On the morning of the flight, Lindbergh arrived at the hangar[3] at 3 a.m. The *Spirit of St. Louis* weighed 5,250 pounds. It had a top speed of 130 mph and a capacity of 400 gallons of fuel. It had a range of 4,000 miles. It was 3,500 miles from New York to Paris.

---

1   wheel out: 推出
2   cruise, *v*: 平穩行駛
3   hangar, *n*: 飛機庫

It was raining when Lindbergh got into the cockpit, buckled[1] his seat belt, and adjusted his goggles. Men pushed on the wing struts[2] to get the plane moving. The wheels were up briefly. Then, the *Spirit* splashed in a mud puddle. Then, the plane was up for good, and Lindbergh pulled back on the throttle[3]. He was on his way. It was 7:54 Eastern Daylight Time, May 20, 1927.

At 9:30 a.m., the small silver plane cleared Rhode Island. The Atlantic Ocean lay ahead. Lindbergh was used to flying over land, guiding himself by landmarks. Now, there would be miles of ocean waves below him.

To save weight, Lindbergh rejected a radio. All he had was a compass, a sextant[4], and a chart. He relied on the stars overhead to guide him.

---

1   buckle, *v*: 扣緊

2   strut, *n*: 支柱

3   throttle, *n*: 節流閥

4   sextant, *n*: 六分儀

After passing over Newfoundland, Lindbergh leveled off at 10,500 feet. He grew very cold. Sleet[1] was pelting[2] the plane. He could see that the wings were icing over. Lindbergh dropped altitude slowly to melt the ice. Thunderheads[3], like huge white mountains, lay before him.

He wove his little plane carefully through the clouds. Lindbergh was assailed[4] by strange feelings. He was not sure if he was asleep or awake. He had to fight to stay awake.

At the 18th hour of the flight, Lindbergh passed the point of no return. It would now have taken longer to go back to New York than to fly on to Paris. Lindbergh had brought along five sandwiches for the journey: two with ham, two with beef, and one with egg. They were all wrapped in grease-proof

---

1   sleet, *n*: 雨雪

2   pelt, *v*: 猛擊

3   thunderhead, *n*: 積雨雲

4   assail, *v*: 困擾

paper. But, he had no appetite. He did not even feel thirsty.

Lindbergh stared at his instrument panel and was struck with confusion. He flexed[1] his muscles, stamped his feet, and bounced in the cockpit to revive himself. He leaned from the cockpit and let the cold air whip him. Whenever Lindbergh started to fall asleep, the plane rattled[2]. This startled[3] him awake.

In the 27th hour, Lindbergh saw something below; perhaps it was land or a boat. He dropped altitude until he was only fifty feet above some fishing trawlers[4]. He was excited to see people after so many hours alone. Lindbergh shouted to them and waved, but they made no sign in return.

An hour later, Lindbergh saw many people below. At first he did not trust

---

1   flex, *v*: 活動

2   rattle, *v*: 發出聲音

3   startle, *v*: 使驚嚇

4   trawler, *n*: 拖網漁船

his own eyesight. Then, he realized he was going across the southwest coast of Ireland. People from the village below looked up and waved.

In the 31st hour, he flew over Cornwall, England. Then, he flew across the French coast. He passed over Cherbourg Harbor at 9:52 p.m. Charles Lindbergh saw the famous Eiffel Tower and the lights of Paris. He had made it.

The *Spirit of St. Louis* set down at LeBourget Airfield in Paris in the darkness of Saturday, May 21, 1927. Charles Lindbergh had flown from New York to Paris in 33 and 1/2 hours. It was 10:24 p.m. European time.

From out of the darkness, Lindbergh heard his name being chanted[1]. What the young American pilot did not yet realize was that his life would never be

---

1   chant, *v*: 高唱

normal again. He had no idea of the price he would have to pay for his courageous deed. His personal privacy was gone. He had opened the world of aviation to the world by crossing the Atlantic. Now, the world wanted to own him.

The wildly enthusiastic crowds caught sight of the handsome, young American with the shy, endearing[1] grin. Their reaction was near hysterical[2]. He was celebrated in the capitals of Europe and surrounded by adoring[3] fans.

Charles Lindbergh, now called "The Lone Eagle," finally returned to the United States. When he arrived, there was one of the largest parades New York had ever seen.

---

1 endearing, *adj*: 令人喜歡
2 hysterical, *adj*: 狂亂
3 adoring, *adj*: 敬慕

Fame caused danger 難逃一劫

Charles Lindbergh received two million pieces of fan mail. Five thousand of the letters contained poetry written about his flight. He also received gifts. Streets, towns, mountains, and newborn babies were named after him. He had become the most famous young man on earth.

Congress voted to give him the Medal of Honor. In the summer of 1927, he made an air tour of the United States in the *Spirit of St. Louis*. Everywhere he went, cheering crowds followed him.

Lindbergh already had contracts with oil and spark plug[1] companies and Wright Aeronautical Corporation. He was offered thousands to endorse[2] other products. Young ladies flocked to the handsome, unmarried Lindbergh.

Up until this point, Lindbergh had never even been on a date with a girl. He was shy and uncomfortable around them. Soon Lindbergh became annoyed with all the attention. A shy loner by nature, he was being grabbed and touched by strangers.

The relentless[3] attention made him sick of being a hero. He just wanted to get back to promoting aviation and getting the spotlight off himself. But it was no use.

---

1   spark plug: 火星塞

2   endorse, *v*: 代言

3   relentless, *adj*: 不停

Most of 1927, Lindbergh spent talking to airline officials about setting up regular commercial airline service. He went to a dinner with President Calvin Coolidge. There, he met Republican Dwight Morrow and his family, including his three daughters. One of the girls, dark haired Anne, took special notice of Lindbergh. He, on the other hand, did not seem to see her at all.

Later, Lindbergh flew to Mexico and stayed with the Morrows. Dwight Morrow was now ambassador to Mexico. This time, Lindbergh did notice petite[1] Anne Morrow. She had a tiny figure. She was obviously intelligent and lively.

Anne Morrow wrote in her diary after the dinner that she liked Charles Lindbergh. But she really did not

---

1   petite, *adj*: 嬌小

believe such a celebrated[1] hero would ever take an interest in her. Still, she began reading *Popular Aviation*. She took a plane ride on the outside chance that Lindbergh would ask her out.

On October 3, 1928, Lindbergh called the Morrow house. He made a date with Anne. He took her for a ride in his plane, and he promised to teach her to fly.

The courtship[2] went quickly. In February 1929 Anne Morrow and Charles Lindbergh were engaged. They were married, May 27, 1929, in Englewood, New Jersey.

Anne and Charles Lindbergh were very different people. She was well read, a good writer, and a lover of music. Lindbergh had never read a book that was not about aviation. Anne was more

---

1   celebrated, *adj*: 有名
2   courtship, *n*: 追求期

well educated than Charles, but they were very much in love.

Anne Lindbergh was determined to please her husband. She flew regularly with him, learning to work the radio and read charts. By the middle of 1929, she was a qualified navigator and radio operator*, and then a pilot.

On June 22, 1930, the Lindbergh's first child, Charles Augustus Lindbergh III, was born. There was incredible interest in the baby, like there was about everything related to Lindbergh.

Lindbergh began to hate the *press* because they were always prying into[1] his life. It was impossible for him to move around without news people following him. He also worried that all this publicity was dangerous for the baby. His fears were justified.

1　pry into: 窺探

In early 1932 Anne Lindbergh was expecting her second child. The Lindberghs lived in Hopewell, New Jersey, on a large secluded[1] estate.

On the evening of March 1, a Tuesday, the family was following its normal routine. The nurse put baby Charles to bed in his crib on the second floor. Charles Lindbergh had arrived home. He was downstairs working when the nurse came running to him.

The nurse had gone to the nursery at 10 p.m. and had found the crib empty. She thought Anne Lindbergh had taken the child, but she had not. Now, the nurse told Charles Lindbergh that his son was missing.

The Lindberghs began a frantic[2] search for Charles to no avail[3]. Then, on the windowsill of the baby's room, they saw an envelope. It was a ransom note. The baby had been kidnapped.

---

1   secluded, *adj*: 隔絕
2   frantic, *adj*: 狂亂
3   no avail: 無用

A new life in Europe 歐洲新生活

A terrible nightmare had begun for the Lindberghs. They paid the ransom, but the baby was not returned. For seventy-two heartbreaking days, the police followed false leads. There was even harassing mail arriving at the Lindbergh home.

Then, on May 12, 1932, a truck driver stumbled upon the body of a small child in a field. Charles Lindbergh went to the morgue[1] to identify the body of his son. The child's head had been crushed.

---

1   morgue, *n*: 停屍間

The Lindberghs were devastated[1] by the tragedy. They were then subjected to[2] a storm of press attention. On August 16, 1932, Anne Lindbergh gave birth to her second son, Jon.

In 1934, Bruno Richard Hauptmann, was arrested for the murder of the Lindbergh baby. He was a German-born carpenter from the Bronx. It was believed that he used a stepladder to kidnap the child. He then may have accidentally dropped Charles while climbing down the ladder. The baby must have been struck in the head, and he died instantly.

In January 1935 a six week trial was held. Charles Lindbergh attended every day. Hauptmann was found guilty and condemned to[3] death.

---

1   devastate, *v*: 打擊
2   subject to: 使受到
3   condemn to: 判罰

The kidnapping and murder of Charles Lindbergh III had a profound[1] effect on Charles Lindbergh. Everything he had always hated and feared about living his life in the full spotlight of publicity had now cost him his son. His darkest fears had come to pass. His fame made him subject to endless press stories. Hauptmann had undoubtedly been inspired by them to kidnap the baby.

All Charles Lindbergh wanted now was to take his wife and newborn son away from the United States. He wanted to take them to peaceful seclusion somewhere else. On December 22, 1935, the Lindberghs sailed from New York on a passenger ship bound for Europe.

---

1 profound, *adj*: 深度

Charles Lindbergh and his wife, Anne.
查理斯・林白與夫人安妮。

In 1936 Bruno Richard Hauptmann was executed. The Lindberghs now lived in England. There, they felt cozy and safe. The English people were more reserved. They did not approach Lindbergh on the street as Americans had done. The press[1] kept its distance as well.

---

1   press, *n*: 新聞界

Charles Lindbergh was then contacted by a United States Army official with a request. Germany, under Adolf Hitler, was rearming[1] very quickly. Her military might was growing so much that other European countries and the United States were worried. Many feared another world war could be on the horizon.

Lindbergh was asked to go to Germany and inspect the German Air Force, the Luftwaffe*. He would go as an honored guest. But, he was asked to keep his eyes open and report back what he saw. The Germans, aware of Lindbergh's fame, were delighted to welcome him.

*Cultural Note

Luftwaffe：納粹德國的空中軍團，在第二次世界大戰初期，是世界上最先進及強大的空軍。納粹德國以先進的戰機主宰了歐洲的天空。

1　rearm, *v*: 重新武裝

CHAPTER 6

Non-intervention 反對美國參戰

On July 22, 1936, Charles Lindbergh was the guest of honor in Germany. For nine days, he toured the country looking at airplane factories. He was very impressed by the advances made by German aviation. He believed the Luftwaffe was an awesome[1] force.

Lindbergh also liked the orderly society he found in Germany. The press was considerate and respectful. Lindbergh was pleased with everything he saw in Germany.

---

1 awesome, *adj:* 使人畏懼

Lindbergh had gone to Germany to find out if the developing war machine posed[1] a threat to the rest of the world. He came away with the belief that Germany was very strong. He thought that it was so strong that engaging it in a war would be a terrible mistake.

In the fall of 1937, Lindbergh returned to Germany and became even more convinced of Germany's great power. He returned to England to convince the British to avoid conflict with Germany.

In 1937 the Lindberghs' third son, Land, was born. Lindbergh was spending most of his time *campaigning* for peace. In August, Lindbergh visited Russia. He hated the communist system being used in Russia. He was not impressed by Russia's military or anything else he saw there.

---

1   pose, *v*: 造成

In 1938 at Munich, Britain appeased[1] Adolf Hitler by giving in to his demands for more land. Charles Lindbergh thought it was the right thing to do. He was becoming more and more pro-German to the shock and dismay of many of his friends.

Hitler had been persecuting the Jews and other minorities for some time. Brutal concentration camps were being built. Eventually, millions would die there. Most people outside Germany believed Hitler was an evil man and a danger to humanity. Lindbergh did not see any of this.

In October 1938 Hermann Goering decorated Charles Lindbergh with the Service Cross of the German Eagle. He was decorated[2] for his contribution to aviation. Goering was a Nazi leader and founder of the savage[3] Gestapo secret police*.

1　appease, *v*: 使滿足
2　decorate, *v*: 授予勳章
3　savage, *adj*: 殘忍

Lindbergh was very upset to find many people in England preparing for war. Lindbergh believed the Nazi regime[1] in Germany had some good points. He felt Germany was justified in invading Czechoslovakia. He also thought Germany was an important barrier to the spread of communism.

Charles Lindbergh learned that people in the United States were also preparing for war with Germany. He was anxious to return home. He wanted to explain to the Americans how useless it was to fight a powerful enemy like Germany. But Lindbergh was worried about how he would be greeted[2] in the United States. He knew that many people were bitter about his pro-German attitude.

Lindbergh left his family in Paris and returned alone to the United States. He wanted to make sure it was safe before he brought his wife and children home.

---

1 regime, *n*: 政權
2 greet, *v*: 對待

He landed in New York in 1939 and had a meeting with President Franklin Roosevelt. The two men distrusted one another. Roosevelt believed war with Germany was inevitable. Lindbergh believed that such a war must be avoided at all costs.

In June 1939 Lindbergh brought his family home. They lived in Lloyd Neck, a secluded part of Long Island, New York. Lindbergh then was on temporary active duty as a colonel in the U. S. Army Air Corps.

In September 1939 Hitler invaded Poland. England and France went to war against Germany.

President Roosevelt was shocked that even now Lindbergh was making speeches urging the United States not to get involved in the war. Lindbergh believed Germany would defeat Britain. To Lindbergh, it did not matter to the

United States who won. After the war, the United States could just make friends with the winner.

Lindbergh resigned[1] from the U.S. Army Air Corps. He made a radio address urging neutrality[2] for the United States. The German army was entering Paris. The Luftwaffe was bombing Britain.

In 1940 the Lindberghs' first daughter, Anne, was born. Lindbergh joined the America First Committee. It was an organization fighting to keep the United States neutral.

Lindbergh spoke to the Congress. He wanted to urge them to turn down the Lend Lease Bill*. The bill was for sending war materials to help England and other countries fighting Germany.

In April 1941 President Roosevelt held a press conference. He said Charles Lindbergh would never be called to

*Cultural Note

Lend Lease Bill： 第二次世界大戰期間，美國根據1941年制訂的租借法案（Lend Lease Bill），對盟國提供物資援助，如飛機、彈藥、軍需品、糧食等。

---

1   resign, *v*: 辭職
2   neutrality, *n*: 中立

active service because of his opinion that Germany was going to win the war.

Roosevelt compared Lindbergh to men who had become traitors during the Civil War. Roosevelt had doubts about Lindbergh's loyalty. The president ordered an investigation of Lindbergh. Lindbergh was watched constantly to see who he was talking to and what he was doing.

In May 1941 Charles Lindbergh made a speech saying that Jewish interests were pushing the United States into the war. This brought a storm of criticism against Lindbergh. Many of his closest friends and admirers turned against him.

On December 7, 1941, Japanese planes attacked Pearl Harbour*[1] in Hawaii. The debate about whether or not the United States would go to war ended with that attack.

---

1   harbour, *n*: 海港，美 harbor

A secret mission 秘密任務

Charles Lindbergh was broken-hearted by the turn of events. He fought hard to keep America at peace, but now he wanted to fight for his country. He offered his services to the army.

He was sent to Secretary of War Stimson. Stimson told Lindbergh that President Roosevelt considered him unfit for service because of his pro-German sentiments[1]. A saddened Lindbergh looked for other ways to help with the war effort.

---

1   sentiment, *n*: 情緒

The Lindberghs' fourth son, Scott, was born in 1942. Around that time, Lindbergh received a call from automobile tycoon[1] Henry Ford. Ford had shared Lindbergh's passion to keep the United States out of the war.

Ford had a large auto factory at Willow Run in New York. The government had asked him to convert production there from cars to military materials. Ford asked Lindbergh to help him turn the plant into a B-24 bomber producer. Ford wanted to do this as quickly as possible.

Charles Lindbergh worked with Ford. Soon, the Willow Run plant was turning out B-24 bombers at an astonishing pace. Then, Charles Lindbergh found a way to join in the war effort without President Roosevelt knowing about it.

---

1   tycoon, *n*: 大亨

Lindbergh's friends from the United States Navy conspired[1] to sneak him into[2] the South Pacific war theater as a civilian technical assistant. President Roosevelt was not told. It would be a secret mission.

On May 8, 1944, Lindbergh landed in the South Pacific. All he was carrying was a shaving razor, soap, boot polish, chocolate bars, a toothbrush, underwear, and a copy of the Bible.

Lindbergh's job was to train other American pilots to fly the Corsair planes in combat against the Japanese in their Zero planes. Lindbergh got aboard one of the Corsairs with a .45 automatic pistol in his gear. He was not authorized to take part in military action. But he had to be ready for whatever happened in this war zone.

---

1   conspire, *v*: 密謀
2   sneak into: 潛入

During the flight, the pilot flying Lindbergh's plane strafed[1] Japanese military camps with machine gun fire. Soon, Lindbergh was firing too. He flew on dawn patrols. He also helped rescue downed pilots over the jungle and in the open sea.

He always asked to get into the front lines. The Marines found out that he, a civilian technical assistant, was actually firing weapons in combat. The Marines winked at[2] it and looked the other way.

On May 29th, Lindbergh dropped a five-hundred-pound bomb on a Japanese aircraft position. He was an expert bombardier[3].

---

1   strafe, *v*: 掃射
2   wink at: 默許
3   bombardier, *n*: 投彈手

Combated Japan 攻擊日本

In the weeks that followed, Charles Lindbergh flew more combat missions than an average combat pilot. He dive-bombed enemy positions, sank barges[1], and patrolled.

Just about every Japanese anti-aircraft gun in Western New Guinea had shot at him. Lindbergh logged[2] twenty-five combat missions and ninety hours of combat time.

On July 10, 1944, he was told that General Douglas MacArthur* wanted to

*Cultural Note

General Douglas MacArthur：道格拉斯・麥克阿瑟將軍，著名軍事家，第二次世界大戰時期歷任美國遠東軍司令，西南太平洋戰區盟軍司令。

1　barge, *n*: 駁船
2　log, *v*: 記錄

see him in Australia. During their cordial[1] meeting, MacArthur asked Lindbergh to return to New Guinea to teach pilots how to reduce fuel consumption. This would enable combat flights to last longer.

On July 28, 1944, Charles Lindbergh joined the 433rd Fighter Squadron[2] as an observer. The mission was to bomb and strafe Japanese positions. Soon, Lindbergh's plane was under attack.

Lindbergh fired for several seconds, watching his shells zoom through the air. But he seemed to be on a collision course with a Japanese fighter plane. As the Japanese plane neared, Lindbergh pulled back on his controls with all the strength he had.

There was a great jolt[3]. The two planes had just five feet of air between them. Lindbergh had managed to avoid the

---

1 cordial, *adj*: 友善
2 squadron, *n*: 中隊
3 jolt, *n*: 撞擊

collision by his manoeuvre[1]. He watched the Japanese plane fall from the sky into the sea. Lindbergh had gotten his first enemy plane.

Lindbergh did not boast[2] about the kill or his skill in saving the plane. He quietly said he shot in self defense and said little else.

Days later, Lindbergh was again in combat when a Japanese Zero *dove down*[3]. The Zero fired at the tail of Lindbergh's plane. Lindbergh crouched behind the armor of the plane and expected to die. But another American plane's bullets shot down the Zero.

Friends tried to talk Lindbergh into[4] returning to the States, but he insisted his job was not yet done. He went to Kwajalein and instructed fighter pilots in long range cruising missions. Once

---

1   manoeuvre, *n*: 策略，[美] maneuver

2   boast, *v*: 自吹自擂

3   dove down: 俯衝

4   talk into: 說服

more he flew in combat. Lindbergh met again with MacArthur. He complimented Lindbergh on the Zero he had gotten.

In September 1944 Lindbergh flew over the Japanese held atolls[1] of Taroa, Maloelap, and Wotje. He carried the heaviest bomb load ever put in a F4U. On September 13th, he dropped the bomb on Wotje Island, destroying a Japanese gun position.

With the end of World War II in sight, Charles Lindbergh ended his combat missions. He headed home. During the time Lindbergh was flying, President Roosevelt never learned that he was fighting. After all, Lindbergh was the man he had deemed[2] unfit to wear an American uniform. But Lindbergh was serving gallantly in the most dangerous war zones.

---

1   atoll, *n:* 環礁
2   deem, *v:* 視為

A military man again 重返軍隊

The last Lindbergh child, a daughter, Reeve, was born in the fall of 1945. The Lindberghs moved to a secluded woodland[1] in Scotts Cove, Connecticut. Charles Lindbergh was able to enjoy his five children. He read to them, invented games for them, and taught them to fish, sail, and hike.

He was a demanding father. He made the children perform their chores to his satisfaction. Anne Lindbergh was a much gentler parent.

---

1   woodland, *n*: 林地

All during the Lindbergh marriage, Charles Lindbergh was often away. Because of this, Anne Lindbergh struggled with loneliness. She wrote poems and essays expressing some of her feelings. She began having her articles and poetry published in major magazines.

Charles Lindbergh also turned to writing in the late 1940s. He wrote *Of Flight and Life,* published in 1948. He described some of his flying experiences. He said that he had come to understand the horrors of Nazi Germany.

He also warned against the spread of Russian communism which was causing great anxiety at the time. He urged a return to basic spiritual truths rather than a complete reliance on science.

Lindbergh always had a deep pacifism

in his heart. He flew combat missions and bombed targets. But he was sad to realize he was taking life[1]. With the publication of his book, Lindbergh's popularity grew. Even those people who were critical of his attitude before World War II had a better understanding of his reasons.

Charles Lindbergh was awarded the Wright Brothers Memorial Trophy in 1949. The twenty-fifth anniversary of Lindbergh's historic flight in the *Spirit of St. Louis* was in 1952. But he refused to take part in any of the commemorations[2]. His strong desire for privacy was still dominant[3]. He did not want the searchlight of the press to find him again.

In 1952, Lindbergh published his second book, *The Spirit of St. Louis.* It told the story of the flight in 1927 and

---

1   take life: 殺生

2   commemoration, *n*: 紀念儀式

3   dominant, *adj*: 最重要

many later events in his life. The book became a best seller. It did even more to restore Lindbergh's reputation. In 1954 he was awarded the Pulitzer Prize* for the book.

*Cultural Note

Pulitzer Prize： 普立茲獎。普立茲獎是美國新聞界的諾貝爾獎，除新聞類獎項以外，也設立另一個類別的獎項，即文學、戲劇及音樂類獎項。這個類別又分為小說、戲劇、歷史、傳記、詩歌、非小說和音樂七項榮譽。

Lindbergh's plane, the Spirit of St. Louis
林白的飛機，聖路易精神號

Also in 1954, President Dwight Eisenhower approved the restoration of Lindbergh's military status. Lindbergh was honored for his contribution to aviation and his great combat service in the South Pacific during World War II. He was made a Brigadier General[1] in the United States Army. In the same year, he was awarded the Daniel Guggenheim Medal for contributions to the nation.

In 1955 Anne Morrow Lindbergh also published a memorable[2] book. During her many years of reflection, she had written down her thoughts. They became *Gift from the Sea*. The small book became an even greater best seller than her husband's book. It remains a classic.

Charles Lindbergh was now working as a troubleshooter[3] for the United States Air Force. His vast knowledge of

---

1 Brigadier General: 準將

2 memorable, *adj*: 難忘

3 troubleshooter, *n*: 檢修員

aviation was used in the development of the nation's rocketry[1] and space programs.

In 1927 Charles Lindbergh had flown over the entire United States, looking down at the beautiful landscape. Many times before, he had made similar flights. But, he increasingly noticed how civilization was moving in on nature. He became troubled by this.

Charles Lindbergh had always loved aviation. But now he began to wonder if the technology he had done so much to advance had really helped humanity.

In September 1962 the Lindberghs were warmly welcomed to the White House by President John F. Kennedy. They spent the night in the Queen's Room at the White House. Lindbergh was deeply moved by the president's graciousness and Jacqueline Kennedy's warmth.

---

1   rocketry, *n*: 火箭研究

A daring pioneer 開拓者先鋒

Charles Lindbergh joined the World Wildlife Fund out of his concern for vanishing species and the damaged environment. He traveled all over the world to see the effects civilization had on the natural environment.

He visited Africa, Indonesia, and South America. He joined in campaigns[1] to save specific endangered[2] animals. These animals included the great blue whales, the giant land tortoises, and

---

1 campaign, *v*: 參加運動
2 endangered, *adj*: 瀕臨滅絕

other species. He became passionate about saving native peoples, animals, birds, plants, and trees.

Lindbergh spent a lot time with the Tasaday tribe in the Philippines. It was a small tribe that lived on the island of Mindanao. They had become objects of curiosity and were threatened with the loss of their way of life.

Lindbergh landed among the Tasadays from a helicopter. He spent some time living with them in a steep mountainside cave. These cave people had not changed their way of life since the dawn of history, and Lindbergh observed how happy they were. The jungle supported them. When he asked them if they needed anything, they could not come up with a request.

Through Lindbergh's efforts, the Tasaday area was named a national reserve. It was banned from outside interference.

Lindbergh fell in love with Hawaii. He bought a small house in Maui. In 1970 he published another book, *The Wartime Journals of Charles A. Lindbergh.* The book revived some of the controversy[1] of the wartime years. He said that the world was now threatened by dangerous communism. He stubbornly pointed out that this was because of the removal of the German barrier to Russian communism.

In the fall of 1973, Charles Lindbergh, who was always very healthy, suffered from a rash and fever. The ailment[2] was at first described as shingles[3]. But then he got a nagging[4] cough that would not go away. He went to the doctor and was diagnosed with advanced lymphatic[5] cancer.

---

1 controversy, *n*: 公開辯論 4 nagging, *adj*: 長期不癒

2 ailment, *n*: 不適 5 lymphatic, *adj*: 淋巴

3 shingles, *n*: 帶狀疱疹

Charles Lindbergh had no fear of death. Throughout his life, he had not been a regular churchgoer. But, in later years, he became interested in religion. He went to a Benedictine monastery in Pennsylvania for solace[1] in 1970. He returned there several times, deeply affected by the spirituality.

Lindbergh wanted to die at home. In the same way that he carefully arranged other parts of his life, he now planned his funeral. He returned to Maui and had a coffin made from eucalyptus[2] wood. He decided he would be buried in a drill shirt and pants.

He chose a burial site in the churchyard. He selected the minister who would read during the service. For about ten days, Charles Lindbergh grew weaker.

---

1   solace, *n*: 慰藉

2   eucalyptus, *n*: 桉樹

During that time he said his farewells to his children and his wife. He double checked his will to make sure everything was in order. On the morning of August 26, 1974, Charles Lindbergh died. Rev. Tincher, who presided[1] at the brief ceremony, described Lindbergh's death as just a new adventure.

Charles Lindbergh, as a very young man, launched the aviation age. His courageous, solo flight across the Atlantic Ocean in 1927, opened the era of commercial aviation. Aviation had been seen as a hobby of daring stuntmen. But then it was accepted as a future means of transportation for humanity. Throughout Lindbergh's life, he advanced the cause of aviation. He also contributed to the space program.

---

1   preside, *v*: 主持

Lindbergh's opposition to America's entrance into World War II* was seen as very wrong. This was especially so because of the enormous evil of Nazi Germany. Lindbergh was a brave combat pilot in World War II. But in his heart, he despised war. He believed that in the end, it accomplished nothing.

He refused to change his position, even though it almost cost him his reputation. Although he passionately opposed the war, he almost died many times fighting for his country. He was far older than most other pilots. He could have easily avoided the danger of combat.

In his later years, Charles Lindbergh remained a pioneer. He pointed out the real dangers of the destruction of the environment. He fought against rampant[1] technology and for endangered species.

1　rampant, *adj*: 未受約束的

He dared to ask the question of whether the aeronautical[1] world, for which he had given his life, had really helped or hindered[2] mankind. He left it for others to answer the question.

Charles Lindbergh, as a young man, helped launch the aviation age.
查理斯・林白於青年時期為開創航空時代作出貢獻。

---

1   aeronautical, *adj*: 航空學

2   hinder, *v*: 妨礙

Exercises 練習

I Vocabulary 詞彙

1.1 Specialized vocabulary 專業詞彙

飛機機師談到航機飛行時往往用他們的專業詞彙，將以下每一個字寫出其定義，有些多於一個定義，只需記下跟飛機和飛行有關的就可以。

1. throttle   _____

2. strut   _____

3. sextant   _____

4. hangar   _____

5. controls   _____

6. parachute   _____

7. aviation   _____

8. instruments   _____

9. aeronautical   _____

10. biplane   _____

11. compass   _____

12. cockpit   _____

13. goggles   _____

14. navigator   _____

1.2 Label groups 分類標示

這些字有那些相通的地方？

May   June

都是一年中的月份。

下面每組字或詞有甚麼相通之處，可以加上適合的字或詞。

1. What do these words have in common?

 England   Germany Russia   _____

 _____

2. What do these words have in common?

 Atlantic Ocean Lake Erie Caribbean Sea _____

 _____

3. What do these words have in common?

 sheep   hogs   cattle   _____

 _____

4. What do these words have in common?

 Paris   New York San Diego _____

 _____

5. What do these words have in common?

 wing   propeller wheel   _____

 _____

6. What do these words have in common?

 Democrat Socialist Green   _____

 _____

7. What do these words have in common?

 motorcycle airplane car   _____

 _____

2 Initial understanding 初步理解

2.1 Cause and effect 因果關係

一個事件的發生總有其原因，結果又有單獨一種原因。

因	果
Lindbergh was tall and lanky.	He was nicknamed "Slim".

以下每個句子，凡屬因的底下畫一條線，屬果的底下畫兩條線。

1. Charles did not like going to school because he did not get along with the other students.

2. Lindbergh was the first person to cross the Atlantic Ocean alone in a plane, and for this, he was awarded the Medal of Honour.

3. President Roosevelt believed that Lindbergh could be a spy for the German military, so he had Lindbergh investigated.

4. According to Lindbergh, animals were going extinct because humans were occupying so much space on Earth.

Answer Key 答案

Part 1 Albert Einstein

I Vocabulary

I.1 Word ladders

compass, mattress, matter, batter
light, tight, time, climb
China, chin, violin, violate
path, math, make, mistake

I.2 Word Scramble

Answers will vary

1. theory; thesis
2. relative; associated
3. physics; forces
4. pacifist; peaceful
5. molecule; atom
6. ponder; consider
7. photon; packet of light
8. frail; weak
9. project; plan
10. advocate; supporter
11. symptom; warning
12. brain; mind
13. optimistic; hopeful
14. university; college
15. article; paper

Part 2 Charles Lindbergh

I. Vocabulary

I.I Specialized vocabulary

1. **throttle:** a lever used to control the speed of the aircraft

2. **struts:** structural supports

3. **sextant:** a tool that uses the position of stars, the sun, and the moon for navigation

4. **hangar:** a place where an airplane is stored

5. **controls:** devices or levers used to guide a machine, like an airplane

6. **parachute:** a fabric device used to help a person float down safely from a great height

7. **aviation:** the operation of aircrafts

8. **instruments:** devices that function as part of a control system

9. **aeronautical:** having to do with the science of flight and aircrafts

10. **biplane:** an airplane with two sets of wings

11. **compass:** an instrument used to determine direction

12. **cockpit:** the space in an airplane where the controls are located and the pilot sits

13. **goggles:** large spectacles or glasses used to prevent injury to the eyes from strong wind or other dangers

14. **navigator:** a person who determines the course or path of a journey

1.2 Label groups

1. France; they are all countries.
2. Pacific; they are all bodies of water.
3. chickens; they are all farm animals.
4. Chicago; they are all cities.
5. cockpit; they are all parts of a plane.
6. Republican; they are all political parties.
7. truck; they are all vehicles for transportation.

2 Initial understanding

2.1 Cause and effect

1. Effect: Charles did not like going to school, Cause: because he did not get along with the other students.
2. Cause: Lindbergh was the first person to cross the Atlantic Ocean alone in a plane, Effect: he was awarded the Medal of Honour.
3. Cause: President Roosevelt believed that Lindbergh could be a spy for the German military, Effect: so he had Lindbergh investigated.
4. According to Lindbergh, Effect: animals were going extinct, Cause: because humans were occupying so much space on Earth.

Proper names
專有名詞

anti-semitism 反猶太主義

Army Air Corps
陸軍航空隊

Aryan 雅利安人

atomic bomb 原子彈

Bern 伯爾尼

Brigadier General 準將

Brownian motion 布朗
運動

Cherbourg Harbour 瑟堡港

Cold War 冷戰

Columbia University
哥倫比亞大學

communism 共產主義

Coolidge, Calvin
柯立芝,卡爾文

Curtiss Jenny
珍妮,寇蒂斯

$E=mc^2$ 質能方程式

Einstein Institute of
Mathematics
愛因斯坦數學研究所

Einstein, Eduard
愛因斯坦,愛德華

Einstein, Elsa
愛因斯坦,艾爾莎

Einstein, Hans Albert
愛因斯坦,漢斯·艾拔

Einstein, Hermann
愛因斯坦,赫爾曼

Einstein, Maja
愛因斯坦,瑪雅

Einstein, Rudolf
愛因斯坦,魯道夫

Eisenhower, Dwight
艾森豪,德懷特

Evolution of Physics
物理學的進化

Ford, Henry 福特,亨利

German Annals of Physics
德國物理活動年報

Goering, Hermann
戈林,赫爾曼

Grossman, Marcel
格羅斯曼,馬塞爾

Hauptmann, Bruno Richard
豪普特曼,布魯諾李察

Hebrew University
希伯來大學

Hiroshima 廣島

Hitler, Adolf
希特拉,阿道夫

Hopewell, New Jersey
厚普維爾鎮,新澤西州

Jewish 猶太人

Kaiser Wilhelm Institute
威廉皇家研究所

Kennedy, Jacqueline
堅尼地,積琪蓮

Kennedy, John F.
堅尼地,約翰·F

Koch, Pauline 科赫,保玲

Lindbergh III, Charles
Augustus
林白三世,查理斯奧古
斯都

Lindbergh, Anne
林白,安妮

Lindbergh, Anne Morrow
林白,安妮莫羅

Lindbergh, Charles
林白,查理斯

Lindbergh, Evangeline
林白,伊文捷琳

Lindbergh, Jon
林白,喬恩

Lindbergh, Land
林白,蘭德

Lindbergh, Reeve
林白,里夫

Little Falls High School
小瀑布市高中

Little Falls, Minnesota
小瀑布市,明尼蘇達州

Luftwaffe 納粹德國空軍

Luitpold School
魯伊特珀勒特學校

MacArthur, General
Douglas
麥克阿瑟將軍,
道格拉斯

Manhattan Project
曼克頓計劃

Maric-Einstein, Mileva
馬利奇—愛因斯坦,
米列娃

Morrow, Dwight
莫羅,德懷特

Nagasaki 長崎

Nazi 納粹

Nazi Party 納粹黨

Nebraska Aircraft
Corporation
內布拉斯加州航空公司

New Guinea 新幾內亞島

Orteig Prize 奧泰格獎

Orteig, Raymond
奧泰格,雷蒙德

patent office 專利局

Pearl Harbour, Hawaii
　　珍珠港，夏威夷

photon 光子

Princeton Hospital
　　普林斯頓醫院

Princeton University
　　普林斯頓大學

Prussian 普魯斯

Prussian Academy of
　　Science
　　普魯斯科學院

Redondo Union High
　　School
　　麗浪多聯合高中

Roosevelt, Franklin
　　羅斯福，富蘭克林

Ryan Aircraft Company
　　瑞恩航空公司

Sidwell Friends School
　　西德韋爾友誼學校

Swiss Federal Polytechnical
　　Institute
　　瑞士聯邦理工學院

the *Spirit of St. Louis*
　　聖路易精神號

Theory of Relativity
　　相對論

Ulm 烏爾姆

Unified Field Theory
　　統一場論

University of Berlin
　　柏林大學

University of Prague
　　布拉格大學

University of Wisconsin
　　威斯康辛大學

University of Zurich
　　蘇黎世大學

Weizmann, Chaim
　　魏茲曼，查姆

Winterthur 溫特圖爾

Zionist 猶太復國主義者

General Vocabulary
一般詞彙

accomplish 實現

adopted 入籍

adoring 敬慕

advocate 提倡者

aeronautical 航空學

ailment 不適

ally 聯盟國

annals 活動年報

appease 使滿足

artery 動脈

assail 困擾

atoll 環礁

atom 原子

autopsy 驗屍

aviation 航空

awesome 使人畏懼

backer 贊助者

barbaric 野蠻

barge 駁船

belittle 貶低

big bang 宇宙大爆炸

biplane 複翼飛機

blast 爆炸

boast 自吹自擂

bombardier 投彈手

brew 形成

brisk 凜冽

buckle 扣緊

cadet 後補軍官

campaign 參加運動

campus 校園

captivate 吸引

carol 聖誕頌歌

casualty 傷亡

celebrated 有名

chant 高唱

chore 零工

chunk 厚塊

coachman 馬車夫

cockpit 駕駛室

colourful 生動，
　　美 colorful

come along 出現

come up with 提出

commemoration 紀念儀式

communist 共產主義者

compass 指南針

condemn to 判罰

conspire 密謀

controversy 公開辯論

cool off 冷卻

courtship 追求期

cordial 友善

cremate 火化

cruise 平穩行駛

cut back on 減少

daredevil 膽大

daring 無畏

decent 足夠

decorate 授予勳章

dedicated 專注

dedicate to 專注於…

deem 視為

deflect 使轉向

deliver 發表

devastate 打擊

dietary 與飲食有關

diligently 勤勉

discipline 紀律
divorcée 離婚者
dominant 最重要
dove down 俯衝
down to earth 務實
draft 徵兵
earn a living 謀生
embitter 激怒
endangered 瀕臨滅絕
endearing 令人喜歡
endorse 代言
eucalyptus 桉樹
exotic 外國
far from 遠非
flare 加劇
flex 活動
frail 虛弱
frantic 狂亂
gifted 有天賦
gravity 重力
greet 對待
hangar 飛機庫
harbour 海港，
　　美 harbor
hinder 妨礙
hot temper 急躁的脾氣
hysterical 狂亂
immensely 非常
inferior parietal 下頂葉
in peril 處於險境
jigsaw puzzle 拼圖
jolt 撞擊
lame 跛
lanky 瘦長
launch 開啟

livestock 家畜
log 記錄
loom 逼近
lymphatic 淋巴
manoeuvre 策略，
　　美 maneuver
marksman 神槍手
memorable 難忘
middle class 中產階層
military parade 閱兵
molecule 分子
morgue 停屍間
mounting 上升
mourn 哀悼
nagging 長期不癒
neutrality 中立
no avail 無用
nonviolence 非暴力
notepad 記事本
optimistic 樂觀
pacifism 和平主義
pacifist 和平主義者
patent 專利
pelt 猛擊
pepper 接連提問
petite 嬌小
physicist 物理學家
physics 物理學
pole 撐船
ponder 琢磨
popular with 受歡迎
pose 造成
preside 主持
press 新聞界
prestige 聲望

prestigious 有聲望
profound 深度
pry into 窺探
pulley 滑輪
rage 猛烈持續
raise 籌募
rampant 未受約束
rattle 發出聲音
rearm 重新武裝
regime 政權
relentless 不停
report card 成績單
Republican 共和黨人
resign 辭職
robust 強壯
rocketry 火箭研究
root 原籍
round 巡迴路線
rugged 健壯
savage 殘忍
secluded 隔絕
sentiment 情緒
sextant 六分儀
shingles 帶狀疱疹
sleet 雨雪
sneak into 潛入
solace 慰藉
spark plug 火星塞
squadron 中隊
startle 使驚嚇
strafe 掃射
strut 支柱
stunt 特技
subject to 使受到
symptom 症狀

synagogue 猶太教堂

take life 殺生

take part in 參與

talented 有才能

talk into 說服

tamper with 擾亂

tarantula 狼蛛

thrill 激動

throttle 節流閥

thunderhead 積雨雲

total eclipse of the sun
　　日全食

trawler 拖網漁船

treacherous 危險

troubleshooter 檢修員

turn …upside down
　　帶來革新

tycoon 大亨

upstart 傲慢的新人

venture 經營項目

verify 證實

war bond 戰時公債

waste-paper basket
　　廢紙筒，美 wastebasket

wheel out 推出

woodland 林地

work with 從事…工作

Timeline of Albert Einstein
艾拔 · 愛因斯坦年表

Events in the life of Albert Einstein

March 14, 1879	Albert Einstein was born in Ulm, Germany. 艾拔・愛因斯坦生於德國的烏爾姆。
1902	Albert Einstein got a job in Bern, Switzerland, at the patent office as a third class examiner. 艾拔・愛因斯坦找到瑞士伯爾尼的專利局任職三級檢查員。
1905	Einstein published a number of research papers that changed science forever. 愛因斯坦公佈了許多永遠改變科學的學術論文。
1909	Einstein became a professor of physics at the University of Zurich. 愛因斯坦成為蘇黎世大學的物理學教授。
1916	Einstein published his ideas as the "General Theory of Relativity." 愛因斯坦公佈了相對論的概念。
April, 1921	Einstein won the Nobel Prize in physics. 愛因斯坦獲得諾貝爾物理獎。
1933	The Einsteins moved permanently to the United States. Einstein was invited to become a professor at Princeton University in New Jersey. 愛因斯坦獲邀擔任新澤西州普林斯頓大學的教授。
1939	Einstein wrote a letter to President Roosevelt describing how an atomic bomb could be produced. 愛因斯坦寫了一封信給羅斯福總統，描述原子彈的製造原理。
May, 1945	Albert Einstein learned of the bombing of Hiroshima, Japan. 艾拔・愛因斯坦得知原子彈在日本廣島爆炸。
April 19, 1955	Albert Einstein died in the Princeton Hospital. 艾拔・愛因斯坦於普林斯頓醫院逝世。

Events in the life of Charles Lindbergh

February 4, 1902	Charles Augustus Lindbergh was born in Detroit, Michigan. 查理斯・奧古斯都・林白出生於密支根州的底特律市。
February 1922	Charles quit college and joined the Nebraska Aircraft Corporation. He worked on planes. 查理斯輟學，加入了內布拉斯加航空公司，他安裝飛機。
1922	In the summer, Lindbergh flew all over the United States on his own plane. He took passengers for rides to earn money. 夏天，林白坐上了自己的飛機遊遍美國，他載客賺錢。
1926	Lindbergh heard of the Orteig Prize. Raymond Orteig was offering $25,000 to any flier or group of fliers who could cross the Atlantic Ocean from New York to Paris non-stop. 林白聽聞奧泰格獎，雷蒙德・奧泰格賞 2 5,000 美元予任何能不停站由紐約飛越大西洋，到達巴黎的飛行員或組別。
May 21, 1927	Lindbergh had flown from New York to Paris in 33 and 1/2 hours. He had opened the world of aviation to the world by crossing the Atlantic. 林白從紐約飛到巴黎，用了 33½ 個小時。通過穿越大西洋這一舉動，他為世人開啟了航空學的里程。
1936	Lindbergh was asked to go to Germany and inspect the German Air Force, the Luftwaffe. He would go as an honoured guest. 林白被要求往探德國空軍的實力，他是以貴賓的身份去的。
July 22, 1936	Lindbergh believed the Luftwaffe was an awesome force. 林白感到納粹德國的空軍實力強橫。

October 1938	Lindbergh believed the Nazi regime in Germany had some good points. Lindbergh was making speeches urging the United States not to get involved in the war. 林白相信德國政權有它值得人稱善的地方。林白發表演説，力勸美國不應捲入戰爭當中。
April 1941	President Roosevelt compared Lindbergh to men who had become traitors during the Civil War because of his opinion that Germany was going to win the war. 因為林白發表德國終贏得戰爭的言論，被羅斯福總統比作為內戰時期的賣國者。
December 7, 1941	Japanese planes attacked Pearl Harbour in Hawaii. 日本襲擊夏威夷的珍珠港。
1942	Lindbergh found a way to join in the war effort without President Roosevelt knowing about it. 林白發現得以投入戰爭而不被羅斯福總統得悉的方法。
May 1944	Lindbergh landed in the South Pacific. His job was to train other American pilots to fly the planes in combat against the Japanese in their Zero planes. He then dive-bombed enemy positions, sank barges, and patrolled. 林白登岸南太平洋，他的工作是訓練美國機師與日軍零式機作戰時，怎樣駕駛飛機。
1952	Lindbergh published his second book. It told the story of the flight in 1927 and many later events in his life. The book did even more to restore Lindbergh's reputation. 林白出版他第二本書，訴説了 1927 年飛行的故事，以及很多他其後生活的事件，這書進一步恢復林白的聲譽。
1960s	Lindbergh visited Africa, Indonesia, and South America. He joined in campaigns to save specific endangered animals. 林白訪問非洲、印尼和南美洲，他加入拯救瀕臨絕種動物的運動。
In the fall of 1973	Lindbergh was diagnosed with advanced lymphatic cancer. 林白被診斷得了淋巴癌。
August 26, 1974	Lindbergh died. 林白過世。

More to Read 延伸閱讀

Abraham, Carolyn. *Possessing Genius: The Bizarre Journey of Einstein's Brain.* New York: St. Martin's Press, 2002.

Berg, A. Scott. *Lindbergh.* New York: G.P. Putnams Sons, 1998.

Kaku, Michio. *Albert Einstein: How Albert Einstein's Vision Transformed Our Understanding of Time and Space.* New York: W.W. Norton, 2004.

Mosley, Leonard. *Lindbergh: A Biography.* Garden City: Doubleday and Co. Inc., 1976.

Overbye, Dennis. *Einstein in Love: A Scientific Romance.* New York: Viking, 2000.